D1497603

GREAT ILLUSTRATED CLASSICS

THE ADVENTURES OF TOM SAWYER

Mark Twain

adapted by
Deidre S. Laiken

Illustrations by
Pablo Marcos Studio

BARONET BOOKS, New York, New York

GREAT ILLUSTRATED CLASSICS

edited by
Malvina G. Vogel

Contents

Mark Twain

About the Author

Mark Twain was born Samuel Langhorne Clemens in a small Missouri town in 1835. After piloting river steamers along the Mississippi for four years, he began writing humorous short stories for newspapers.

The Adventures of Tom Sawyer was Twain's first full-length novel. Many of thee adventures of Tom and Huck Finn actually happened to Twain in his boyhood.

Even though Twain wrote this book mainly to entertain boys and girls, he hoped that adults would read and enjoy it, and recall their own childhood.

Mark Twain died in 1910. But he left the world a true picture of American life and the American spirit in his novels, short stories, and other writings.

Sid Tells About Tom's Mischief.

CHAPTER 1
The Great Whitewash

Tom Sawyer was always getting into trouble. He was the kind of boy who just could not resist adventure.

Tom lived with his Aunt Polly, his cousin Mary and his half-brother Sid. Everyone was used to Tom's mischief, but Sid never missed a chance to tell Aunt Polly when he thought Tom was up to no good. That's how she found out that Tom was playing hooky from school and going swimming.

Now, as a punishment for his behavior, Tom found himself faced with the chore of whitewashing 30 yards of fence on a sunny Saturday afternoon. And what was worse—it was one of those warm summer days when everyone else was out playing ball or swimming. And there was Tom, all alone on the sidewalk with a long-handled brush and a bucket of whitewash.

He looked at the fence. It seemed enormous, and he knew it would take all day to give it only one coat. Tom began to think of all the fun he had planned for this day, and his sorrows multiplied. Soon his friends would come down the street, and he shuddered to think of how they would laugh to see him whitewashing a fence on such a beautiful day. There must be a way out of this situation.

Tom emptied his pockets and looked at his worldly wealth—bits of toys, marbles, and trash. He might be able to bribe someone else to help him for a while, but there wasn't

A Fence to Be Whitewashed

nearly enough to buy a whole day of freedom. Tom thought for a while . . . then an inspiration burst upon him!

He picked up the brush and began to spread the whitewash slowly and peacefully over the fence. In only a few minutes, Ben Rogers came walking by, eating a big, juicy red apple. Tom's mouth watered at the sight of such a treat, but he kept on painting and pretended not to see or hear Ben at all.

"Hey there, Tom, what's up with you?" called Ben. "It's too bad you have to work on a day like this. I'm just on my way to the river for a swim. Too bad you can't come along!"

Tom looked at Ben for a moment, then said, "What do you call work?"

"Why, ain't that work?" asked Ben, pointing to the fence.

"Well maybe it is, and maybe it ain't," answered Tom. "All I know is that it suits me

Ben Wants Tom to Go Swimming.

just fine."

"Come on now, don't tell me you actually *like* it!"

"*Like* it? Well, I don't see why I shouldn't like it. It isn't every day that a boy gets to whitewash a fence."

That puts things in a new light for Ben. He stopped eating his apple and began watching Tom work. Maybe there was something to this whitewashing after all, he thought.

"Hey, Tom, let me try it for a while," Ben asked.

"No, no!" protested Tom. "Aunt Polly entrusted this fence to me, and I can't just let anyone take over such a big job."

But Ben continued to beg Tom to let him have the privilege of whitewashing for just a little while. Tom kept refusing until Ben offered him the rest of his juicy red apple. That had been what Tom was waiting for.

Tom sat in the shade and munched the ap-

An Even Exchange

ple while Ben swished the brush back and forth, sweating at his work. It was a wonderful idea, and as other boys came by, Tom kept trading with them too.

By mid-afternoon, the fence was completely whitewashed, and Tom was the proud owner of all sorts of treasures. His inspiration had certainly worked. All he had to do was make his chores seem to be fun, and the other boys were eager to do them for him.

When the fence was completed, Tom went into the house. "Can I go out and play now, Aunt Polly?" he asked.

"What! Already? How much have you done?"

"It's all finished, Aunt Polly."

"Tom, don't lie to me. I can't bear it," she warned.

"Look for yourself," answered Tom as he led his aunt to the window.

"Well, I never!" exclaimed Aunt Polly.

"Look for Yourself."

"You really *can* work when you put your mind to it."

She was so pleased with Tom's work that she presented him with a large juicy apple and told him he could go out, but to be home in time for dinner. Tom smiled, and when she turned her back, he slipped a sugar-coated doughnut into his left pocket.

Within minutes, Tom was out on the street as free as a bird. As he passed the house where Jeff Thatcher lived, he saw a girl in the garden—a new girl he had never seen before. She was lovely. Her blonde hair fell in two long braids almost to her waist. Tom fell in love instantly!

He tried to attract her attention by standing on his head and showing off in all sorts of silly ways, but she ignored him. Tom vowed that before the week was up he would win her love. He skipped down the street, his head full of romantic plans and adventures.

The Girl Ignores Tom.

A Loose Tooth

CHAPTER 2
Tom Meets Becky

It was Monday morning and Tom Sawyer was miserable. He was always miserable on Monday mornings because it meant he had to go to school. Tom began to scheme. There had to be a way, some way, to avoid going to school. He could be sick and stay home. But as much as he tried, Tom could not find the least little thing wrong with himself.

He thought for a little while longer and then realized that one of his upper front teeth was loose. This was really a lucky break. Just as he was about to begin groaning and writhing in pain, he remembered Aunt Polly's way of pulling loose teeth, and Tom was in no hurry to suffer *that* particular pain again.

So he went back to thinking. He remembered hearing the doctor describe an illness that had laid up a patient for two weeks and threatened to make him lose a finger. Tom had a sore toe—something he hadn't looked at or thought about in days. Now he wondered if he could possibly fool Aunt Polly. Since he didn't know the details about the illness, he figured a few loud cries of pain might do the trick. So Tom began to groan and moan with considerable spirit.

Sid, who lay sleeping in the next bed, did not even stir. Tom increased the volume and frequency of his cries, but his half brother snored on. Finally, Tom shook Sid until his sleepy eyes opened in surprise. Tom began to groan again.

"Tom! What's going on?" shouted Sid.

Tom Moans and Groans.

"Oh, don't jump around so," moaned Tom.

Despite Tom's protestations, Sid ran downstairs to tell Aunt Polly about Tom's apparent agony.

"I . . . I think he's dying," stammered Sid.

"Rubbish! I don't believe it," snapped Aunt Polly. But she ran up the stairs as fast as she could. By the time she reached Tom's bedside, her face was white with fear.

"What's the matter with you, Tom?"

"Oh, Aunt Polly, it's my sore toe. It feels as if it's about to fall off."

Aunt Polly sank into a chair with relief. She laughed a little, then cried a little, and then did both together. This made her feel so much better that she snapped at Tom, "Stop this nonsense, get out of bed, and get off to school immediately!"

All this made Tom feel quite foolish, and he stopped his awful groaning immediately.

"Oh, Aunt Polly," he said, "it just hurt so

"I . . . I Think He's Dying."

much I never minded my tooth at all."

No sooner were the words out of his mouth than Aunt Polly was carefully examining the loose tooth. In minutes, she had tied a loop of silk thread to the tooth and the other end of the thread to the bedpost. Tom pleaded with Aunt Polly not to pull it this way, but it was no use. She left the room, only to return moments later with a hot log from the kitchen stove. She thrust the log dangerously close to Tom's face. He jumped back and gazed in horror at the tooth dangling by a thread from the bedpost.

On the way to school, the obvious gap in Tom's front row of teeth attracted the attention and envy of all the other boys. Maybe the pain was worth it after all, thought Tom.

As he neared the school, he came upon Huckleberry Finn. Huck was the son of the town drunkard and was free to come and go as he pleased. He was always dressed in cast

Pulling Tom's Tooth

off clothes and incredible rags. He slept in doorways or empty barns and never had to go to school or church. In short, Huck was the envy of every boy in town, but he was treated as an outcast by their mothers.

Tom waved to Huck, and the two boys got involved in a serious conversation about the best way to cure warts. Then Huck showed Tom a tiny tick that he had managed to capture. Tom's eyes lit up at the sight of the little creature, and he made a quick trade—his tooth for the tick.

This little transaction made Tom late for school, and when he entered the classroom, Mr. Dobins, the teacher, demanded an explanation.

Tom was about to concoct a wonderful lie when he noticed the lovely girl with the long blonde braids. Tom also noticed that the only empty desk in the room was on the girls' side, next to this mysterious beauty.

Huck Finn Shows Tom His Tick.

Without a moment's hestitation, Tom answered, "I was with Huckleberry Finn."

Everyone in the class gasped! Even the teacher was astonished. No one would ever actually admit being with the town renegade. In an instant, the teacher brought out the switch of hickory twigs and whipped Tom as a punishment. Then he ordered Tom to sit with the girls. This, of course, was exactly what Tom wanted. He quickly slid into the empty seat next to the new girl.

Tom tried desperately to attract her attention. He offered her a lovely ripe peach, but she only tossed her head and looked away. Next, Tom began to draw something on his slate. He covered his work with his hand and appeared to be very involved in this activity.

Soon, the girl's curiosity got the best of her, and she made an attempt to see the drawing. But Tom kept on working and pretended to be totally unaware of her attentions. At last,

A Switch of Hickory Twigs

she gave in and hesitatingly whispered, "Let me see it!"

Tom partly uncovered a drawing of a house with a brick chimney and smoke curling into a blue sky. The girl's interest grew. Soon she asked Tom to draw in people.

"It's such a nice drawing," she said. "I wish I could draw."

"It's easy," whispered Tom. "I'll teach you."

The girl told him that her name was Becky Thatcher. Tom and Becky agreed to spend the lunch recess together, with Tom teaching her how to draw.

Tom went back to his drawing, but this time he hid the slate from Becky. She begged to see it, but he refused. Finally, he gave in and showed Becky the slate. The words "I love you" were printed in Tom's own steady handwriting. Becky blushed, but anyone could see she was pleased.

"It's Such a Nice Drawing."

Tom Watches the Tick.

CHAPTER 3
Heartbreak for Tom

Tom thought that the lunch recess would never come. The air in the classroom was utterly dead. Not a breath was stirring. It was the sleepiest of sleepy days. It took all of Tom's strength just to stay awake. His hand wandered into his pocket, and he pulled out the tiny matchbox which held the tick he had traded his tooth for. Tom released the creature and watched it crawl along the long, flat desk.

Joe Harper, Tom's best friend, sat next to him. Joe, too, was grateful for the diversion of a tick on such a dull Monday. Tom poked at the tick with a pin, and the creature changed his direction at every poke. Joe took a pin out of his lapel and joined in the sport.

In a few minutes, Tom complained that they were interfering with each other, and neither was getting the fullest benefit of the tick. So he put Joe's slate on the desk and drew a line down the middle. One side was to be Tom's territory and the other side, Joe's.

The poor tick scurried from one tormentor to the other, and the two boys bent their heads over the slate, giving all their attention to the game. It didn't take long before they began to argue, and Tom reached over into Joe's territory and poked the tick with his pin.

"Tom, you let him alone!" shouted Joe.

"Look here, Joe Harper, just whose tick is it anyway?" answered Tom.

The boys were so involved in their game

A Fine Game

that they didn't notice the hush that had come over the class. They didn't realize that Mr. Dobins had tiptoed towards them and was now standing and watching their game. Before they knew it, they felt the harsh smacks of hickory twigs on their shoulders. The punishment ended their game.

When school was let out for lunch, Becky was waiting for Tom. The two walked off together to a secret place in the yard behind the school.

For a while, Tom drew on his slate as Becky, obviously impressed, watched him in silence. After some time, Tom looked up and asked, "Were you ever engaged, Becky?"

"I don't know," she answered. "What's it like to be engaged?"

"Well, you just tell a boy that you won't love anyone but him, ever, and then you kiss. Anyone can do it."

At first, Becky hesitated, but Tom ex-

A Punishment at Hand

plained over and over again the importance of the kiss and the pledge of undying love.

When Becky agreed, Tom kissed her. Then he relaxed and told her of the rest of the agreement.

"We'll always walk to school together, and at parties you choose me and I choose you. We'll always be together, when nobody is looking, that is."

"It's so nice. I never heard of being engaged before," whispered Becky with a sigh.

"Oh, it's a lot of fun! Why me and Amy Lawrence . . ."

Becky's wide eyes filled with tears, and Tom realized he had made a terrible mistake. He tried to comfort Becky and explain that he had no feelings for Amy anymore. But Becky would hear none of it. She turned her face to the wall and went on crying.

Tom got up and walked around the school-yard for a while. Then he returned to Becky's

An Engagement Kiss

side and once again told her that she was his only love. But Becky kept on crying.

Tom reached into his pocket for his most important treasure—a brass doorknob. He passed it to Becky and said, "Please, Becky, won't you take it?"

Becky threw the doorknob on the ground.

Tom got up and stomped out of the school-yard. He headed for the hills outside of town and didn't return to school at all that afternoon.

Becky soon regretted her actions and began looking for Tom everywhere. She called his name over and over, but there was no answer. She had no companions but silence and loneliness, so she sat down to cry again.

As the rest of the students filed back into the school, Becky looked hopefully for some sign of Tom, but it was too late. Her heart was broken, and she was sure she had lost him forever.

Tom Offers His Treasure to Becky.

Life Is Pain and Trouble.

CHAPTER 4
Tragedy in the Graveyard

Tom ran through the back roads until he was far away from the dreaded schoolyard. He sat for a long time by the side of the road with his elbows on his knees and his chin in his hands. It seemed to him that life was nothing but pain and trouble. He had only meant the best for Becky Thatcher. What had he done that was so terrible? Nothing!

She had treated him like a dog. Oh, she would be sorry some day—maybe when it was too late!

Tom's mind wandered to thoughts of death.

He could almost see it all now. They would carry his poor body into the church, and Becky and Aunt Polly would cry and cry. They would say all sorts of kind things about what a brave, wonderful boy he had been all along.

Tom was awakened from his fantasy by his old friend, Huckleberry Finn. The boys were overjoyed to see each other and began to play a lively game of Robin Hood.

When Tom realized that it was close to dinner time, he said good-bye to Huck. But they made arrangements to sneak out that night and meet in the graveyard, where they planned some more adventures.

At half past nine that night, Tom and Sid went to bed as usual. Tom waited for what seemed like eternity for Huck's signal that the coast was clear. Finally, Tom heard the "meow" that meant Huck was waiting down by the woodshed.

Overjoyed to See Each Other

Tom opened the window, slipped out, and joined his friend. Huck was waiting with his dead cat, for they planned to swing it over a grave to see if this method would cure warts.

The boys walked about a mile and a half out of the village until they reached an old graveyard on a hill. Grass and weeds grew over the grounds, and many of the older graves were so sunken in that the gravestones could not be seen at all.

"Huck, do you believe that these dead people would like us being here?" whispered Tom.

"I wish I knew. It's awful solemn, isn't it?" answered Huck.

Just then, Tom thought he heard something. He grabbed Huck's arm and the two boys froze.

"Did you hear it?" asked Tom. "There's something coming this way, no doubt about it!"

Tom Slips Out to Meet Huck.

Some shadowy figures approached through the gloom. One was swinging an old-fashioned tin lantern. Huck shuddered and whispered, "It's the devils, sure enough. Three of them. We're goners now, Tom, can you pray?"

Just as Tom was about to begin praying, he recognized one of the figures. "They're humans!" he whispered. "One of them, anyway. It's old Muff Potter. I know his voice."

The boys sat very still watching the three figures standing over a grave. The lantern light revealed their faces. It was young Dr. Robinson, Muff Potter, and fearsome Injun Joe, a murderer.

Potter and Injun Joe were unloading some rope and shovels from a wheelbarrow. Dr. Robinson stood beside them, urging them to hurry and dig open the grave before the moon came out.

After a while, their shovels struck something with a dull, woody sound. They hoisted

Shadowy Figures in the Graveyard

a coffin out of the ground with their ropes, pried off the lid, and removed a body. The corpse was placed in the wheelbarrow and covered with a blanket.

"Now it's done," said Injun Joe with a grunt. "Five more dollars or here it sits."

The doctor protested, "But I paid you both in advance."

But Injun Joe had been carrying an old grudge against the doctor's father ever since the old man had him jailed for threatening his life. Now, he raised his fist to the doctor's face.

Dr. Robinson struck out suddenly and knocked Injun Joe to the ground. Muff Potter jumped on the doctor, and the two men began to fight. In an instant, Injun Joe was on his feet. Wild fire was in his eyes. He snatched up Potter's knife and crept around the fighters, seeking his chance to use it.

At the moment the doctor freed himself

The Fight!

from Potter's strong grasp, Injun Joe picked up a heavy tombstone and knocked out Potter with it. Then he drove his knife into the doctor's chest. The doctor reeled and fell on top of Potter. His blood was everywhere.

Injun Joe stood looking down at his two victims. The doctor groaned, gave a last gasp, and then was still. Injun Joe knelt down and went through the doctor's pockets for money and other valuables. Then he placed the fatal knife in Potter's open right hand.

In a few minutes, Potter came to. His hand closed upon the knife. He raised it, glanced at it, and dropped it with a shudder.

"Lord, how did this all happen?" he cried.

Injun Joe then told Muff Potter that he had seen the whole thing. "Potter," he explained, "you were so drunk that you got into a fight with the doctor and wound up stabbing the poor man to death."

At first, Potter refused to believe what In-

Injun Joe Frames Potter.

jun Joe had told him. But Injun Joe was so convincing, that Potter eventually accepted the story as true and begged his partner to keep it a secret. When this was agreed upon, the two men slipped silently away into the night. The murdered doctor, the blanketed corpse, the lidless coffin, and the open grave were all that remained of the night's terror.

The two boys fled back towards the village, fearful of every shadow and speechless with horror.

"Huck, what do you think will happen?" Tom whispered breathlessly.

"If Dr. Robinson dies, I guess there will be a hanging," answered Huck in between gasps for air.

Then both boys realized that they had been the only witnesses to the crime. Muff Potter had been out cold. Only Huck and Tom could point an accusing finger at the real killer. It was then that they understood the great dan-

Tom and Huck Flee.

ger they were in. Injun Joe was not likely to let them go on living if he suspected that they had seen the murder and might give him away.

Once the boys were safely back in the village, they stopped to talk inside an old ruined building.

"Hucky, do you think you can keep mum about all this?" asked Tom.

"We *got* to keep mum, Tom. That Injun Joe would wipe us out in a minute if we were to squeal. Now listen, Tom, we've got to swear to keep quiet about all this."

The boys agreed. In the darkness of night, they wrote out an oath on a piece of bark. It read: HUCK FINN AND TOM SAWYER SWEARS THEY WILL KEEP MUM ABOUT THIS AND THEY WISH THEY MAY DROP DOWN DEAD IN THEIR TRACKS AND ROT IF THEY EVER TELL.

Then they pricked their fingers and signed

Writing the Oath

their initials in blood. They buried the bark and whispered all sorts of magical words during the ceremony.

Now it was done. The oath had been sealed in blood. Tom and Huck would never tell anyone what they had witnessed that awful night. Their lips were sealed forever!

Sealing the Oath in Blood

Tom Sneaks In—Unnoticed?

CHAPTER 5
Tom and His Guilty Conscience

After the boys said good-bye, Tom returned to his house and crept silently in his bedroom window. He undressed with great care and fell asleep congratulating himself that no one knew of his adventure. He was not aware that the gently snoring Sid was awake and had been so for almost an hour.

When Tom awoke the next morning, Sid was dressed and gone. Something was wrong. No one had bothered to wake him. Within five minutes he was dressed and downstairs, feeling sore and drowsy.

After breakfast, Aunt Polly took Tom aside and wept. He had broken her old heart.

"Go on and ruin yourself," she cried. "It's no use for me to try and raise you like a good boy. I know you sneaked out last night."

Tom pleaded for forgiveness and promised to reform. He was so miserable he didn't even think of ways of getting even with Sid for telling on him. He moped to school, feeling sad and gloomy.

With hardly a sound, he slipped into his seat. His elbow pressed against something hard and cold. He held it up and unwrapped it. A long lingering sigh followed and his heart broke. It was his brass doorknob. Becky had returned it!

Tom hardly had time to wallow in his sorrow. By noontime, the whole village was alive with news of Dr. Robinson's murder. Everyone in town was drifting towards the graveyard. Tom's heartbreak over Becky flew

Tom's Gift Is Returned.

away, and he joined the procession. As soon as he reached the scene of the bloody crime, he felt a slight pinch on his arm. It was Huckleberry Finn. They looked into each other's faces and felt tense and uncomfortable because of the secret they shared.

Within a few minutes, Injun Joe and Muff Potter appeared. Without a moment's hesitation, Injun Joe told the sheriff a grisly tale, calmly explaining that Muff Potter had stabbed the doctor during a drunken rage.

Huck and Tom stood frozen in their tracks as the stony-hearted liar reeled off his story. The boys were astonished. An innocent man was going to hang, and only they could save him.

Tom's fearful secret and gnawing conscience disturbed his sleep that night and every night that followed. After several nights of Tom's moaning and tossing, Sid complained to Aunt Polly. She questioned Tom, but all

A Stony-Hearted Liar!

he said was, "It's nothing, nothing at all."

But Sid, who seemed just a bit too concerned, had to say, "But you talk so much, Tom. Last night in your sleep, you kept screaming something about blood and telling somebody something."

This made Aunt Polly think that Tom was only having nightmares about the murder, just like other people in the town were. Although Tom nodded his head in agreement, Sid suspected that something much more dramatic was bothering Tom.

Every day or two during this time, Tom went to the little jail window and smuggled small gifts to Muff Potter. Cigars and bits of fruit and food were silently passed to the prisoner. Muff thanked Tom and figured it was the boy's way of thanking him for the few times they had gone fishing together. But to Tom, these offerings were the only way he had of easing his guilty conscience.

Tom Eases His Guilty Conscience.

Tom Watches Becky's Window.

CHAPTER 6
The Cat and the Pain-Killer

This was a bad time for Tom Sawyer. Aside from his sleepless nights, he had another problem. Becky Thatcher had stopped coming to school. Tom began finding himself hanging around her house, watching her window, and feeling miserable. He'd heard she was ill. What if she should die!

There was no joy in life for poor Tom. He put away his bat and his ball and dragged himself through each day.

Aunt Polly became alarmed. She had never seen Tom this way. She tried all sorts of homemade remedies on the boy, but nothing seemed to work. Instead of getting better, Tom just seemed to grow paler and more dejected. What bothered Aunt Polly more than anything was Tom's total indifference to all her usual remedies. Ordinarily, he would put up an incredible fuss when he had to swallow medicines, take hot oatmeal baths, or suffer under hot compresses.

Then Aunt Polly heard of "Pain-Killer"—a medicine she saw advertised in a magazine. When it arrived, she tested it. It was horrible! But, at least if Tom complained, he would show some spark of his old self again.

She gave him a teaspoonful and watched for the result. Her fears were instantly put to rest, for Tom showed an unusual interest in the medicine.

What Aunt Polly did not know was that Tom was becoming bored with his unhappy existence. He was also tired of all her at-

An Advertisement for "Pain-Killer"

tempts to nurse him back to health. So he thought of various plans for getting out of this situation. It finally hit him that the best thing to do was to pretend to actually enjoy the "Pain-Killer." He began to ask for it so often that he became a nuisance, and Aunt Polly wound up telling him to simply help himself. Little did she suspect that Tom was pouring the liquid into a crack in the parlor floor when nobody was looking.

One day, when Tom was getting rid of the medicine this way, his aunt's cat, Peter, came into the parlor. Peter eyed the spoon in Tom's hand and seemed to beg for a taste.

"Don't ask for it unless you want it, Peter," said Tom.

But Peter meowed that he *did* want it.

"You better make sure."

Peter was sure.

Tom pried open the cat's mouth and poured down the "Pain-Killer." Peter sprang a cou-

Giving Peter the "Pain-Killer"

ple of yards into the air and let out a loud war whoop. Then he set off around the room, banging against furniture, upsetting flowerpots, and making a mess of the house.

Aunt Polly entered the room and stared in amazement as Peter did a few double somersaults and sailed through the open window, carrying with him the rest of the flowerpots.

Tom lay on the floor laughing so hard he was crying. But he finally did manage to tell his aunt what had made the cat act so crazy. The old woman's face broke into a smile. She had to admit that it was a cruel thing for the boy to have done, but at least it was a sign that Tom had his old lively spirit back.

Peter Acts Crazy.

Becky Won't Look at Tom.

CHAPTER 7
The Pirates Set Sail

Just when Tom's life seemed to be worth living again, misery set in. Becky Thatcher finally returned to school. Tom was overjoyed when he saw her familiar blonde hair and glowing face in the schoolyard. He tried to get her attention by jumping over the fence, yelling, laughing, doing handsprings, standing on his head, and throwing secret glances in her direction. But nothing worked. Becky never even looked at him.

Tom's cheeks burned in shame. He had made a fool of himself. He couldn't stay at school and be miserable, so he gathered his things together and sneaked off.

He walked and walked until the school was only a tiny black speck in the distance. He was gloomy and desperate. Nothing mattered now. He was a friendless, forsaken boy, and nobody cared whether he lived or died.

He was so deep in his misery that he didn't see his old friend Joe Harper heading towards him. Joe looked worse than Tom. He explained that his mother had just punished him for drinking some cream which he had never even tasted. He swore he was completely innocent.

The two boys walked along, spilling out their misery to each other. They made a pact to stand by one another as brothers and never separate till death.

They began to plan some way of escaping from their lives of misery and pain. Joe wanted to be a hermit and live on crusts of

Deep in Misery

bread and water, but Tom had a much more exciting idea. He suggested that they become pirates.

Tom knew of the perfect pirate hideout—a small, uninhabited island out in the Mississippi River called Jackson's Island. He and Joe sought out Huck Finn and invited him to join them on this wild adventure. When Huck agreed, they made plans to meet at a lonely spot on the river bank two miles above the village at midnight. Each would bring fishing hooks and lines and as much food and other provisions as he could steal.

It was a starry and very still night as Tom made his way out of the village. The mighty river lay like an ocean at rest. When Tom reached the bank, he heard nothing, so he gave a low, distinct whistle. It was answered. Both Huck and Joe appeared from behind a bluff. Joe carried a side of bacon, and Huck carried a skillet, a bag of tobacco, and corn-

A Midnight Meeting

cobs from which to make pipes. Tom showed them the boiled ham cakes he had brought.

The boys loaded their provisions onto a small raft tied up on the bank, and they pushed silently away from shore.

About two o'clock in the morning, the raft grounded on Jackson's Island. The boys jumped off, tied the raft to a nearby tree, and set out to gather wood for a fire.

They built their fire against the side of a great log and cooked some bacon for dinner. The climbing fire lit up their faces and threw its ruddy glare on the trees, foliage, and twisting vines.

When dinner was over, the boys stretched out on the grass and fell into a deep, contented sleep.

Tom awoke the next morning wondering where he was. It took a few minutes for him to realize that he had actually run away from home. Joe and Huck were fast asleep. Tom

Reaching Jackson's Island

woke them, and they all began talking excitedly. In a minute or two, they had stripped off their clothes and were chasing each other and tumbling about in the shallow water.

They returned to camp wonderfully refreshed, happy, and very hungry. Soon, Huck had the campfire blazing again. They had a delicious breakfast of coffee, bacon, and fried catfish which Huck had caught.

After filling themselves until they could eat no more, the boys explored the island a bit. They discovered that it was about three miles long and a quarter of a mile wide. The shore that lay closest to the mainland was separated from the island by a narrow channel hardly two hundred yards wide.

The boys took a swim every hour, so it wasn't until mid-afternoon that they finally returned to camp. After feasting on cold ham, they threw themselves down in the shade to talk. But the talk soon began to drag . . . and

A Life of Swimming and Eating

then died. The stillness and the sense of loneliness began to affect the boys.

Soon they all realized that they were truly homesick. Even poor homeless Huck Finn was dreaming of doorways and life back in town. But the boys were all ashamed of their feelings, and none of them was brave enough to utter a word.

Suddenly, the boys became aware of a peculiar sound in the distance. It was a strange, muffled boom.

"Let's go see what it is!" shouted Tom.

They sprang to their feet and hurried to the shore. They parted the bushes on the bank and peered out over the water. A little ferryboat was steaming up the river about a mile below the village, its deck crowded with people. Suddenly, a great puff of white smoke burst from the ferryboat's side, followed by that same dull, booming sound they had heard earlier.

A Great Puff of White Smoke

"I know now!" exclaimed Tom. "Somebody's drowned!"

"That's it!" cried Huck. "They did that last summer when Bill Turner drowned. Now I remember. Folks say that the boom will make a drowned body rise to the surface."

"I sure wish I was over there now," said Joe. "I wonder who it is that drowned."

The boys stood still as they listened and watched. Presently, a thought flashed through Tom's mind, and he shouted, "I know who's drowned—it's *us*!"

They had become heroes in an instant. They were missed. They were mourned. Hearts were breaking because of their running away. The whole town was talking about them. Here was their triumph at last! Being pirates was worthwhile after all.

As twilight drew on, the boat went back to the dock in town, and the pirates made their way back to camp, excited over their discov-

"I Know Who's Drowned—It's *Us!*"

ery.

They caught a fish, fried it over the open fire, and talked all during dinner. Their conversation centered on what people might be saying about them and who was missing them.

But when the shadows of night closed in, they stopped talking and sat gazing into the fire. The excitement was gone now, and Tom and Joe could not help thinking about the people back home who were not enjoying this little adventure at all. They began to have misgivings, and soon they drifted into sad, troubled moods.

Joe was the first to timidly mention these feelings. He asked Tom and Huck how they might feel about returning to civilization. But the two boys only laughed and denied any homesickness at all.

When the fire had died, the boys all turned in for the night—all, that is, except Tom.

Fresh Fish for Dinner

Tom Looks in the Window.

CHAPTER 8
Tom's Visit Home

Tom waited to make sure Huck and Joe were fast asleep. When he was absolutely sure, he tiptoed cautiously among the trees until he was out of hearing. Then he ran straight for the raft on shore.

By ten o'clock, he was back in town. He flew along the streets and alleys and shortly found himself at his aunt's back fence. He climbed over it and looked in through the sitting-room window where a light still burned. Seeing no one inside, Tom went to the door and softly lifted the latch. When the opening was just big enough for him to fit through, he slipped into the sitting room and quickly hid under the bed. From his hiding place, Tom could see two people enter the room, and he could hear Aunt Polly talking.

"But, as I was saying," she cried, "he wasn't bad—only mischevious. He never meant any harm, and he was the best-hearted boy who ever was." She sank down onto the bed and cried.

"It was just like that with my Joe," sobbed the other voice, which Tom recognized as Mrs. Harper's. "He was always full of the devil and up to every kind of mischief, but he was just as unselfish and kind as he could be."

Tom went on listening and realized that everyone assumed the boys had drowned while taking a swim. Then, when the raft was discovered missing, there was hope that they had gone down the river to the next

Talking About the Drowned Boys

town. But when that hope vanished too, the boys were believed to have drowned somewhere in the middle of the river. If the bodies were not found by Saturday, the boys' funeral would be held at noon on Sunday.

Tom shuddered when he heard the news. He watched as Aunt Polly knelt down and prayed for him. The tears fell as she whispered words of love and endearment for him.

After Mrs. Harper had left and Aunt Polly was asleep, Tom crept out from under the bed and stood looking at the old woman by the light of the candle. His heart was full of pity for her. He thought he should write her a note and tell her that he was really alive.

So Tom took a piece of sycamore bark out of his pocket, put it on the table, and began to write. But then he got an interesting idea and quickly put the bark away.

As he started out the door, Tom bent over his aunt and kissed her. He would return another time.

A Kiss for Aunt Polly

Hunting for Turtle Eggs

CHAPTER 9
The Pirates Return

It was morning when Tom finally returned to camp. Huck and Joe were already up and glad to see him. They had begun to worry where he had gone. During a sumptuous breakfast of bacon and fish, Tom recounted his adventure back in the village. When he finished, he hid himself away in a shady nook and slept until noon.

The day passed slowly, with the boys hunting for turtle eggs, fishing from the shore, and swimming until they were tired and ready to rest. A sadness came upon each of the boys, and they fell to gazing across the wide river to the town. Tom found himself writing "Becky" in the sand with his big toe.

Finally, Joe broke the silence. "Oh, let's give it up," he said. "I want to go home. It's so lonesome here."

"Oh no, Joe, you'll feel better soon," said Tom. "Just think of the great fishing that's here."

"I don't care for fishing. I want to go home."

Tom tried again. "But Joe, there isn't another swimming place like this anywhere."

It was no use. Soon, even Huck was convinced that it was time to give up and go home. Tom, however, remained firm; he refused to leave the island.

By this time it was beginning to get dark, so Huck and Joe began gathering their things. They didn't want to leave without Tom, but he absolutely refused to consider giving up and going home.

"BECKY"

"Tom, I wish you'd come too," said Huck. "Now you think it over. We'll wait for you down by the shore."

Tom stood watching as Joe and Huck walked slowly away. Suddenly, an idea hit him and he ran after his friends yelling, "Wait! Wait! I want to tell you something."

Joe and Huck stopped and turned around. When Tom reached them, he began explaining his secret plan. The boys listened quietly until they saw the point he was driving at.

Yes, they agreed, Tom had a wonderful plan, even though it meant they would have to stay on the island four more days until Saturday.

Somehow, knowing that they would be going home soon helped Tom, Huck, and Joe pass those days quickly. They fished, swam, played games, and made plans for their return.

When Sunday finally came, the town was

Tom Has a Wonderful Plan.

mournful and silent. The Harpers and Aunt Polly's family were full of grief. The villagers hardly talked, and there was a strange feeling of sadness in the air.

Becky Thatcher found herself moping around the deserted schoolyard, feeling miserable and talking to herself.

"Oh, if only I had that brass doorknob again!" she murmured. "But I haven't anything now to remember him by." And she choked back a little sob. Becky regretted what she had done to Tom. Now she was sure she would never see him again. Just the thought of this touched her so deeply that tears began to roll down her cheeks.

Nearby, a group of boys talked in low voices about Tom and Joe. They retold stories of their two lost friends and shook their heads in disbelief at the thought that they were really gone forever.

At noon, the church bell began to toll. The

Becky Mourns Tom.

villagers gathered in the church, and only the sound of whispering was heard. No one could remember when the little church had been so crowded. A hush came over the villagers when Aunt Polly entered, followed by Sid and the whole Harper family. As the silent, black-clad procession made their way slowly down the aisle, the whole congregation stood in respect.

The funeral service began with the minister describing the boys in glowing terms. He related many incidents in their young lives, and as he talked, the congregation became more and more moved. Soon, there was hardly a dry eye in the church.

A slight rustling sound in the gallery went unnoticed, but a moment later, the creaking of the church door interrupted the service. The minister raised his weeping eyes and stood transfixed! First one, then another pair of eyes followed the minister's gaze. Then,

The Funeral Service Begins.

almost at the very same instant, the congregation rose and stared at the three "dead" boys marching up the aisle. They had hidden in the gallery and listened to their own funeral sermon!

Aunt Polly and the Harpers threw themselves upon the boys and smothered them with hugs and kisses.

Suddenly the minister shouted at the top of his voice, "Praise God! Sing! And put your hearts into it!"

And the whole congregation did. The sound of their voices shook the rafters, while Tom Sawyer, the Pirate, looked around the church at his friends and confessed in his heart that this was the proudest moment of his life.

Three "Dead" Boys Return!

Tom Tells Sid of His Adventures.

CHAPTER 10
Back Home Again

That was Tom's great secret—the plan to return home with his brother pirates and attend their own funeral. They had paddled over to the town on Saturday and slept in the woods at the edge of the village. At daybreak on Sunday, they crept into the church and finished their sleep in the gallery.

At breakfast on Monday morning, Aunt Polly was very loving to Tom, but he was busy chattering away with Sid about the events of the day before. After a while, Aunt Polly broke in.

"Tom, I don't say it wasn't a fine joke—to keep everybody suffering almost a week so you boys could have a good time. But it was a pity you were so hard-hearted as to let me suffer so. If you could come over to go to your own funeral, you could have come over and given me a hint some way that you weren't dead. I suppose if you really loved me, you would have wanted to do that."

This made Tom feel guilty. He *had* actually come to tell Aunt Polly that he was all right. He had even written her a note telling her just that. But instead of owning up to the truth, Tom made up a story of a dream he had on Jackson's Island.

"I dreamed I was right here in this very room, Aunt Polly. Mrs. Harper was here too. The two of you were crying and saying how much you missed us. I think you were saying how even though we got into trouble, we were always kind-hearted boys."

"You Were So Hard-Hearted."

Tom gave such a perfectly detailed description of that unhappy night that Aunt Polly was truly amazed. This dream seemed to convince her that Tom had a special gift. She was so pleased that she took a big red apple from the cupboard and gave it to him to eat on the way to school.

What a hero Tom had become! He did not go skipping and prancing, but moved with a dignified swagger as became a pirate who felt that the public eye was on him. And indeed it was. Tom tried to ignore the looks and remarks as he passed people, but they were food and drink to him—he was enjoying every moment.

Smaller boys flocked at his heels, and older boys were consumed with envy. They would have given anything to have his swarthy, sun-tanned skin and his sudden fame.

At school, the children made such a fuss over Tom and Joe and gazed at them with

Tom Is a Hero!

such admiration, that the two heroes quickly became "stuck up." They told and retold their adventures to eager listeners who wanted to hear the whole story over and over again.

Tom decided that he could be independent of Becky Thatcher now. His fame and glory were enough. He would live for that alone. Now that he was so distinguished, maybe she would want to make up. Well, let her, he decided. She could try all she wanted.

When Becky arrived at school, Tom pretended not to see her. He moved away and joined a group of boys and girls and began to talk. Soon he noticed that Becky was tripping gaily back and forth, her face flushed and her eyes dancing. She pretended to be busy chasing schoolmates and screaming with laughter.

When Tom pretended not to see her at all, Becky came closer and once or twice glanced wistfully toward him. Soon she noticed that

Tom Is Independent of Becky Now.

Tom was talking more to Amy Lawrence than to anyone else. She felt a sharp pang and grew disturbed and uneasy. In a moment of anger and jealousy, Becky announced that she was planning a party during the vacation. Soon everyone was begging for invitations. Everyone, that is, except Tom and Amy. Tom just turned coldly away and took Amy with him.

Becky's lips trembled and tears came to her eyes. She hid these signs and went on talking gaily. As soon as she could, she sneaked away by herself and burst into tears. She'd think of some way to get even with Tom.

At recess, Tom continued his flirtation with Amy, but only after he'd checked to see if Becky was still watching. When he looked across the schoolyard, he saw something that made his blood boil. Becky was sitting cozily on a little bench looking at a picture book with Alfred Temple. They were so absorbed

Becky Sits with Alfred Temple.

that their heads were almost touching. Jealousy ran red-hot through Tom's veins. He began to hate himself for throwing away the chance Becky had offered for making up. By noon Tom couldn't take it any longer, and he left school and ran home.

Once Becky saw that Tom was no longer around, she lost all interest in Alfred and the picture book. She burst into tears, got up, and walked away.

Alfred ran after her, trying to comfort her, but she snapped, "Go away and leave me alone, can't you! I hate you!"

The boy stopped in amazement and wondered what he could have done. He was humiliated and angry once he figured out the truth. Becky had simply used him to make Tom jealous, but he would get back at Tom. The question was *how*.

Then he thought of the perfect way to do it. He went inside the classroom and found

"Go Away and Leave Me Alone!"

Tom's spelling book on his desk. He opened to the lesson for the afternoon and poured ink all over the page.

At that moment, Becky was glancing in through a window behind him. She saw the whole thing, but she moved on and said nothing. So Becky started on her way home, intending to find Tom and tell him what Alfred had done. She hoped that Tom would be so thankful, that all their troubles would be over.

But before she was halfway home, she changed her mind. She thought back to the way Tom had treated her, and she was filled with anger. Let Tom get punished because of the damaged spelling book, she decided. And she also decided to hate him forever.

Alfred's Revenge!

"I've a Notion to Skin You Alive!"

CHAPTER 11
Aunt Polly Learns the Truth

Tom arrived home in a dreary mood, and his aunt's first words showed him that he had brought his misery to the wrong place.

"Tom, I've a notion to skin you alive!" cried Aunt Polly.

"What have I done?" asked Tom in surprise.

"Done? You've done enough! Here I go over to Mrs. Harper's house like an old softy, expecting to make her believe all that stuff about your dream, and then she tells me that Joe told her the whole truth. You really *were* here and heard the talk we had that night. Tom, I don't know what's to become of a boy who acts like that. It makes me feel so bad to think you could let me go to Mrs. Harper and make such a fool of myself and never say a word."

Tom hung his head for a moment. He had no answer to give his aunt. He could only try to explain that he didn't think it would turn out this way. But his explanation only made Aunt Polly angrier. Finally, Tom gave in and told his aunt that the real reason he had returned that night was to tell her that he really hadn't drowned and to ease her mind.

Aunt Polly looked up sternly and said, "Tom, I would be the thankfulest soul in this world if I could believe that you ever had such a good thought, but you know you never did. And I know it too!"

Tom pleaded and tried to convince his aunt that he really was telling the truth. "When

Tom Explains His Visit.

you and Mrs. Harper got to talking about the funeral," he said, "I just got all full of the idea of our coming and hiding in the church. It seemed like such a terrific plan, I couldn't bear to spoil it. So I just put the bark back in my pocket and kept mum."

"What bark?" Aunt Polly asked.

"The bark I wrote on to tell you we'd gone pirating. I wish now you'd woken up when I kissed you. I do, honest."

The hard lines in his aunt's face relaxed, and a sudden tenderness dawned in her eyes. She couldn't believe that Tom had really kissed her. But she could tell that the boy was speaking the truth. Still, she had to be sure.

When Tom had gone off to school, Aunt Polly ran to the closet and took out the jacket he had worn on the pirating trip. She hesitated before putting her hand in the pocket. If Tom was lying this time, she couldn't bear

Aunt Polly Checks Tom's Jacket Pocket.

it. Twice she put her hand in the pocket and twice she pulled it away. But she could not resist. On the third try, she withdrew Tom's piece of bark and read the note through flowing tears.

"I could forgive the boy now," she cried, "even if he'd committed a million sins!"

Aunt Polly Forgives Tom.

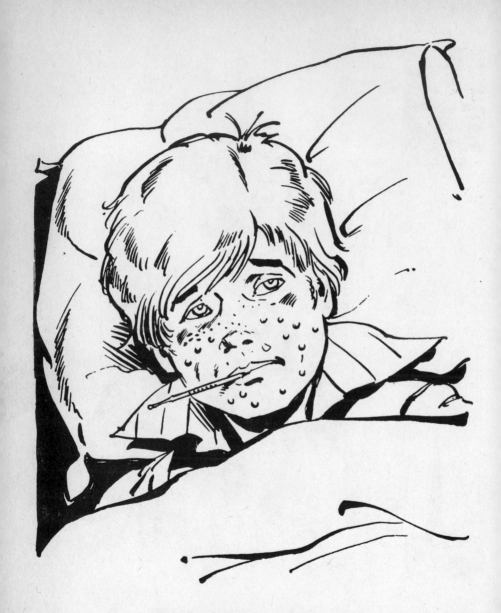

The Measles!

CHAPTER 12
The Salvation of Muff Potter

Summer brought with it the usual adventures, hopes, and disappointments. It was Tom's unfortunate luck to catch the measles, and he had to stay in bed for almost three weeks. Those weeks seemed like an eternity, and when at last he was out again, the whole town was buzzing with excitement.

Muff Potter's murder trial was finally starting. It was the topic of every conversation. Tom could not escape it. Every mention of the murder sent a shudder through him and kept him in a cold sweat all the time.

When he couldn't stand it any longer, Tom looked for Huck. He had to have a talk with him. It would be some relief to unseal his tongue for a little while. In addition, he wanted to assure himself that Huck had kept the morbid secret.

"Huck, have you ever told anybody about . . . *that*?" whispered Tom.

"About what?" asked Huck.

"You know what."

"Oh! Of course I haven't."

"Never a word?"

"Never a solitary word. So help me!"

Tom felt more comfortable, but he insisted that they swear again to keep mum about what they had seen that fateful night.

After Huck and Tom sealed their pact with another oath of blood, they discussed the fate of poor Muff Potter.

"I've heard talk that the people plan to lynch him if the court frees him," said Tom.

Swearing Again to Keep Mum

The boys took a long walk and had a long talk, but it brought them little comfort. As twilight drew on, they found themselves hanging around the neighborhood of the jailhouse. They somehow hoped that something would happen to clear away their problems. But nothing did.

The boys did as they had often done before. They went to the cell grating on the ground floor and gave Potter some tobacco and matches. Luckily, there were no guards around. Muff was always so thankful for their little gifts, that it only made their consciences ache more.

After the visit, Tom went home miserable. That night, his dreams were full of horrors.

Each day during the trial, Tom hung around the courtroom, drawn by an almost irresistible impulse to go in. But he forced himself to stay out. Huck was having the same experiences.

Tom's Nightmare

Finally, the great day came—the day that the jury was to make its decision. The villagers filed into the courtroom and sat waiting for the news. The judge and jury entered and took their places.

Shortly afterward, Potter was brought in. He looked pale and haggard, timid and hopeless. All eyes were on him. Injun Joe sat in the gallery, looking fierce and angry.

Instead of waiting for the jury to reveal its decision, Potter's attorney rose to make an announcement. He had an important new witness and wanted to change Potter's plea to "not guilty."

In a firm clear voice, he said, "Call Thomas Sawyer to the stand."

Looks of puzzled amazement appeared on every face in the courtroom, Muff Potter's included. Every eye fastened itself on Tom with interest as he rose and took his place on the stand. He was scared, but he took the oath

"Call Thomas Sawyer to the Stand!"

without hesitation.

Then the defense attorney asked the fateful question. "Thomas Sawyer, where were you on the seventeenth of June, about the hour of midnight?"

Tom glanced at Injun Joe's iron face, and his tongue froze. The audience waited breathlessly for Tom's reply, but his words refused to come.

After a few moments and a few deep breaths, Tom relaxed enough so that his words began to flow. He told the whole story. He explained why he and Huck had been in the cemetery that night and described every detail of the ghastly murder.

On hearing Tom's story, Injun Joe sprang from his seat, tore his way through the crowd, and leaped through the window.

As a result of Tom's testimony, Muff Potter was set free. But Injun Joe was still alive and out there somewhere, waiting . . .

Injun Joe Escapes!

The Hero!

CHAPTER 13
Digging for Buried Treasure

So once again Tom was a hero and his name even appeared in the village newspaper. Tom's days were filled with happiness and praise, but his nights were dark and terrible. Injun Joe haunted all his dreams, and Tom was too afraid to venture out and meet Huck as he used to do. Poor Huck was in the same state of terror.

The night before the jury was to hand down its decision, Tom had gone to see Muff Potter's attorney and had told him the whole story. Huck was disappointed with Tom for breaking their oath of secrecy, but Tom's conscience could not bear the heavy burden of what he had seen. Now, Tom and Huck were afraid Injun Joe would never be captured. They felt sure that they could never draw a safe breath again until that villain was dead and they had seen his corpse.

Rewards were offered for Injun Joe's capture, and a detective was even hired, but not a clue was uncovered.

The days drifted on, and eventually Tom and Huck began to relax more and more. Soon they were even ready to start on a new adventure.

One afternoon, Tom suggested to Huck that they try digging for buried treasure. Huck was doubtful, but Tom explained that there was treasure all over the place just waiting to be dug up. He described how robbers hid their stolen money under dead trees and in haunted houses. His descriptions were

A Reward for Injun Joe's Capture

so convincing that Huck finally agreed to join him on the hunt.

The boys gathered picks and shovels and began the long, three-mile walk up to Still-House Hill. When they reached the first dead tree, they began to dig. They worked and sweated for half an hour. No result. They toiled another hour. Still nothing.

"Do they always bury it as deep as this?" asked Huck.

"Sometimes, not always," answered Tom "Maybe we just haven't got the right place."

So they found another dead tree and then another and dug some more, but there was no sign of any treasure. Eventually, the boys began to tire. It was at this point that Tom got another idea.

"Let's look in the haunted house on Cardiff Hill," he said.

Huck objected. The house was empty, so everyone assumed it was haunted, but no one

Digging for Buried Treasure

had ever dared to explore it. Tom finally convinced Huck that if any treasure was to be found, it would most likely be in the haunted house.

When they reached the house, there was something so weird and grisly about the silence, that they were afraid, for a moment, to venture in. Then they crept to the door and took a trembling peep. They saw a cobwebbed, floorless room overgrown with weeds. It had an old fireplace and open spaces where windows once were.

Tom and Huck entered on tiptoe, their ears alert to catch the slightest sound. When they heard nothing for several minutes, they relaxed and began to explore the place with interest. In one corner, they found a closet. What mystery did it contain? . . . They turned the knob, the closet squeaked open, and then . . . nothing! The closet was empty.

They were full of courage now and decided

The Haunted House

to explore the second floor. Just as they reached the top of the stairs . . .

"Sh!" said Tom.

"What is it?" whispered Huck.

"Sh! . . . There! . . . Hear it?"

"Yes! . . . Let's run!"

But they didn't dare make a sound by running. They stretched themselves out on the floor, glued their eyes to the knotholes in the rotting wood, and lay waiting in misery and fear.

Two men entered the room below. The boys recognized one as an old deaf-and-dumb beggar who had been around town lately. The other man, a ragged, unkempt creature with an unpleasant face, was someone they had never seen before. The two men began to talk.

"No, I thought it over," said the ragged man, "and I don't like it. It's too dangerous." His voice seemed vaguely familiar to the boys.

Tom and Huck Hear Voices Below.

"Dangerous?" grunted the deaf-and-dumb beggar. "It is not!"

Suddenly Tom and Huck began to shake. The deaf-and-dumb man could hear and speak! But even worse, they recognized the familiar voice. It was Injun Joe's! The boys froze, hardly daring to breathe.

The men talked about plans for another "job," then ate some lunch, and soon fell into a deep sleep.

Huck and Tom decided to take this chance to escape. They rose slowly and softly. But their first step made such a hideous creak on the rotted floor that they sank back down, dead with fright.

They lay there, counting the dragging moments until Injun Joe finally awoke. He kicked his partner in the ribs, and the two men began to count their money. They had nearly six hundred dollars which they decided to bury in the room until they were

Spying on Injun Joe and His Partner

ready to make their escape. So Injun Joe began to rip at the old wooden floor planks with his knife. Suddenly his knife struck something solid.

"What's this?" he muttered as he reached his hand in and pulled out an old rusty box.

The two men pried open the lid, and there before their eyes were hundreds of gold coins and stacks of bills that had to be worth thousands of dollars!

"This must be where old Vic Murrel's gang hid their loot," said Injun Joe.

"What luck!" shouted his companion. "Now you won't have to do that other job."

Injun Joe frowned. "You don't know me," he snapped. "That job isn't just **robbery, it**'s revenge! I'll need your help, **and when it**'s finished, we can leave for good."

Tom and Huck began to **shake even more.** *Revenge!* That could only **mean that Injun** Joe was still after them **for giving testimony**

Treasure!

at Muff Potter's trial.

"Let's hide the loot," said Injun Joe.

"I'll bury it at number two, under the cross," said the beggar.

Injun Joe agreed, and the two men left the house with shovels, picks, and their treasure.

Tom and Huck waited a long time before they dared come out of hiding. They had only two things on their minds—Injun's Joe's revenge and the treasure hidden at number two, under the cross.

"Let's Hide the Loot."

Planning Their Strategy

CHAPTER 14
Trembling on the Trail

The adventure of the day tormented Tom's dreams that night. Even his waking hours were filled with fantasies of the thousands of dollars he and Huck had seen. It was more money than either boy had ever believed possible. If they could only figure out what Injun Joe had meant by "number two, under the cross," the money would be theirs.

The next afternoon, Huck and Tom met down by the river to plan their strategy.

"Huck, I've been thinking," began Tom. "I think that 'number two' might be the number of a room in a tavern."

Huck immediately agreed. This idea sounded reasonable, and since there were only two taverns in town, he decided to find out which one had a room called "number two."

Within an hour, Huck had returned with some information. The smaller tavern had a room which was kept locked at all times. Huck was sure this was the "number two" Injun Joe had mentioned in the haunted house. The boys agreed to stake out the tavern.

They met that night and hid in the alley by the tavern door. No one resembling Injun Joe or his partner entered or left. After several hours, the boys gave up and agreed to return again the next night.

The following evening, at the same hour, they resumed their watch. This time, Huck stood guard, while Tom ventured closer to the

Staking Out the Tavern

tavern and to the locked room.

Huck waited in silence for what seemed like hours. "Maybe Tom fainted," he thought. "Maybe he has been caught. What if he is dead?"

Suddenly, there was a flash of light, and Tom came tearing by him, shouting, "Run! Run for your life!"

Tom didn't need to repeat these words. Huck was practically flying after him. When the two boys reached the abandoned barn at the edge of the village, they relaxed. As soon as Tom got his breath, he explained, "Huck, it was awful! I tried two of my keys, just as soft as I could, but they wouldn't turn. Then I took hold of the knob, and the door opened. It wasn't even locked! As I walked in . . . I almost stepped onto Injun Joe's hand! He was lying there, sound asleep on the floor, with his arms spread out. Huck, I didn't wait to look around. I didn't see the box and I didn't

"Run for Your Life!"

see the cross. All I saw was a lot of bottles and Injun Joe—stone drunk!"

The boys agreed that it was too risky to return to the tavern that night. Instead, Huck promised to watch the place every night, and if Injun Joe or his partner ever left for a while, he would give Tom the signal.

The boys said good night. Tom returned home, and Huck found a deserted hayloft to sleep in.

That night, Tom lay awake thinking of Injun Joe and the treasure and later dreamed of them too. There was no escape from these thoughts!

Huck Finds a Deserted Hayloft.

Tom and Becky, Back Together

CHAPTER 15
Huck Saves the Widow

The next morning, the first thing Tom heard was a piece of good news. Becky Thatcher, who had been on vacation with her family, had just returned. Now, Injun Joe and the treasure sank into secondary importance, and Becky took the chief place in Tom's interest.

He saw her, and they spent the afternoon talking and having a wonderful time together. Becky finally got permission to have the picnic she had planned months ago. The invitations were sent out before sunset, and the next day promised to be a treat for every boy and girl in town.

Tom's excitement kept him awake until a pretty late hour. He had hopes of hearing Huck's signal, but he was disappointed. No signal came that night.

By twelve o'clock the next afternoon, everyone was gathered in the Thatcher's yard to set out for the picnic. They boarded a ferryboat and planned to spend the day picnicking on the other side of the river.

Three miles below town, the ferryboat stopped in a wooded cove and tied up. The crowd swarmed ashore, and soon their laughter and shouts could be heard echoing throughout the forest.

By and by somebody shouted, "Who's ready for the cave?"

Everybody was. Bundles of candles were collected, and everyone scampered up the hillside to the mouth of the cave. It was an

"Who's Ready for the Cave?"

opening shaped like the letter "A." The inside of the cave was romantic and mysterious to explore. People said that one could wander days and nights through its intricate chambers and never get out. Nobody "knew" the cave. That was an impossible thing. Most of the young men knew a portion of it, but nobody ever dared venture beyond this known portion. So Tom knew as little of the cave as anyone did.

The crowd filed into the cave and began the exploration. Laughter and shouts echoed from the walls for an hour. Then the clanging of the ferryboat alerted everyone to the time.

As the ferryboat's lights came glinting towards the wharf in town, one pair of eyes glanced at them in the cloudy, dark night. Those eyes had been glued to the tavern door for hours, but, by now, Huck Finn had just about given up any hope of seeing Injun Joe. Suddenly a noise fell upon his ear. He was

Exploring the Cave

all attention.

Two men brushed by him, and one seemed to have something under his arm. It must be the box! So they were going to move the treasure. Why call Tom now? It would take too much time, and the men would get away. Then the treasure would be lost forever. So Huck decided to follow them himself.

The men moved up the river street three blocks, then turned left up a hill. Huck followed them for what seemed like hours. Soon the men stopped. They were five steps away from the path which led to the Widow Douglas' house.

Huck crept up behind them and heard a very low voice saying, "Drat! Maybe she's got company. I can see lights."

The men began to plot and plan. A deadly chill went to Huck's heart. This was the "revenge" job! Injun Joe still held a grudge against the Widow's dead husband who had

Huck Discovers Injun Joe's Plan.

been a judge and had Injun Joe horsewhipped as a punishment for vagrancy. Now, even though the judge was dead, Injun Joe decided to take his revenge on the old woman. He described horrible tortures he was planning, and as he spoke, he polished his knife. Huck could hear the evil in his voice.

Huck's first thought was to run. Then he remembered that the Widow Douglas had been kind to him more than once. These men were actually planning to murder her! He wanted to warn her, but there was no way to do it without being seen.

Holding his breath, Huck silently slipped away and sped to the nearest house. It was the home of Bill Welsh and his sons. Huck banged at the door.

"What's going on out there? Who's banging? What do you want?" called Mr. Welsh.

Huck breathlessly blurted out the story and begged Mr. Welsh not to tell anyone that

Begging Mr. Welsh to Help

it was him who squealed. He urged the man and his sons to hurry.

Three minutes later, Mr. Welsh and his sons, all well-armed, were at the top of the hill. Huck accompanied them no farther. He hid behind a large boulder and listened. There was a lagging, anxious silence, and then all of a sudden there was an explosion of firearms and a cry.

Huck didn't wait for anything. He sprang away and sped down the hill as fast as his legs could carry him.

At dawn the next morning, Huck returned to the Welsh home. Mr. Welsh and his sons greeted him with a warm welcome and a hearty breakfast. Then he told Huck that the Widow had been saved, but the villains had escaped.

The Welshes Go to Save the Widow.

Lost!

CHAPTER 16
Lost in the Cave

All the while that Huck was following Injun Joe and his partner to the Widow Douglas' house, Tom and Becky were still on the
other side of the shore exploring the cave.
Neither knew that the picnic party had long
since departed. And, in the excitement of
boarding the boat, no one in the laughing,
shouting crowd of young people had noticed
that Tom and Becky were not with them.

Without realizing it, Tom and Becky had
lost their way. They had started through a
long corridor in the cave and, at each new

opening, they glanced to see if it looked familiar. But every time, the path was strange to Tom. His confidence began to fail him, and soon he began turning off into new openings at random. Becky began to cry.

"We're lost, Tom! We'll never get out of here. The others have left, and we'll surely die here before anyone finds us."

Tom tried to cheer her up. He assured her that they would find a way out.

But after several hours, hunger and fatigue set in. They ate their last piece of cake, and Becky's legs refused to carry her another inch. So she and Tom sat down and rested. In the light of their last candle, they talked of home, its comfortable beds, and all their friends. When the candle finally flickered and went out, Becky cried, and Tom frowned in silence. He was frightened too.

Time passed. Tom and Becky fell asleep and woke up several times. They had no way

The Last Food

of knowing how many hours or even days were passing. Only the gnawing hunger in their stomachs reminded them that time was slowly going by.

"Tom, do you think they'll miss us and come and hunt for us?" Becky asked hopefully.

"Yes, they will! They certainly will!" Tom reassured her.

Tom and Becky both realized how worried and anxious their family and friends must be. Their conversation drifted off, and they became silent and thoughtful.

The hours passed, and hunger began to torment them again. They were getting too weak to even move when Tom suddenly gasped. "Sh! Did you hear that?"

They both held their breaths and listened. There was a sound like a faint, far-off shout.

Tom jumped up and quickly answered it. Then he helped Becky to her feet. Leading

"Sh! Did You Hear That?"

her by the hand, he started groping down the corridor in the direction of the shouts. Every few minutes they stopped and listened again. Each time, the sound seemed to be getting closer and closer.

"It's them!" shouted Tom. "They've come for us! Becky, we're all right now!"

The joy of the prisoners was almost overwhelming. Their speed was slow, however, because large, deep pits were common in the cave, and they had to walk carefully. They shortly came to one pit and had to stop. It might be three feet deep, it might be a hundred. They could not pass it.

Tom got down on his stomach and reached down as far as he could. No bottom. They would have to stay there and wait until the searchers came. They listened for the shouts again, but the voices were becoming more and more distant. After a little while, they disappeared altogether.

A Bottomless Pit!

Tom and Becky were miserable. Tom shouted until he was hoarse, but it was no use. Still, he talked hopefully to Becky as they groped their way back to a spring of fresh water they had passed earlier. They lay down to rest there, and the weary time dragged on.

When Tom awoke and could think clearly, he realized that there were some side passages along the corridors. It would be better to explore some of them than to sit and do nothing. So he took a ball of kite string from his pocket, tied it to a rock jutting out from the cave wall, and he and Becky started off. Tom led the way, unwinding the line as he groped along. At the end of twenty steps, the corridor ended in a ledge. Tom got down on his knees and felt below and then as far around the corner as he could reach. The moment his head turned the corner, his heart

Kite String to Mark the Way

filled with joy. For not twenty yards away he saw a human hand holding a candle.

Tom stood up and began to shout. Instantly, that hand was followed by a body from behind a rock. Tom was paralyzed with fear when he recognized . . . *Injun Joe!*

But before Tom could grab Becky and run, Injun Joe fled into the darkness. He probably had not recognized Tom's voice because of the echoes in the cave.

Still, Tom's fright weakened every muscle in his body. He told himself that if he had strength enough to get back to the spring, he would stay there. Nothing would tempt him to risk meeting Injun Joe again. He did not want to alarm Becky by telling her what he had seen, so he explained that he had only shouted "for luck."

But hunger led Tom to try again. After a long sleep, he awoke, ready to explore the cave once more. Becky was very weak. She

Injun Joe!

had sunk into a half-conscious state and would not be roused to go with him. She mumbled that she would wait where she was and die—it would not be long. She told Tom to go with the kite string and explore if he wanted to, but she asked only that he return to stay by her and hold herhand until it was all over.

Tom choked back a sob and kissed her. He made a show of being confident of finding the searchers or an escape from the cave, but he was distressed with hunger and fear. Taking the kite string in his hand, he went groping down one of the passages on his hands and knees.

Desperate for a Way to Escape

Mrs. Thatcher Is Very Ill.

CHAPTER 17
Escape!

Back in the village, everyone was in mourning. It was Tuesday, and the children had been missing for three days. Most of the searchers had given up and gone back to their everyday lives, certain that Tom and Becky would never be found.

Mrs. Thatcher was very ill. People who visited her said it was heartbreaking to hear her call Becky's name, raise her head to listen for an answer, then collapse wearily with a moan.

Aunt Polly had drooped into a depression,

and her grey hair had turned almost white overnight.

On Tuesday, the townsfolk went to sleep, sad and forlorn, only to be awakened in the middle of the night by a wild peal from the village bells. Within moments, the streets were swarming with frantic, half-dressed people shouting, "They're found, they're found!"

Tin pans and horns were added to the din as the villagers gathered and moved toward the river. An open carraige drawn by shouting citizens delivered Tom and Becky into their arms.

The village was all lit up and alive with excitement. It was the greatest night the little town of St. Petersburg had ever seen! During the first half-hour, a procession of villagers filed through the Thatcher house, touching Tom and Becky, kissing them, and trying to speak. But nobody could. Everyone was crying

"They're Found, They're Found!"

with joy and relief.

Aunt Polly's happiness was complete, but Mrs. Thatcher had to get a message to her husband first. He was still out at the cave searching for the children.

Tom lay upon the sofa with an eager audience around him. He told the history of the wonderful adventure, putting in many extra little tidbits to make it even more exciting. He described how he had left Becky and gone on an exploring expedition; how he had followed two passages as far as his kite string would reach; how he had followed the third to the fullest stretch of the kite string; and how he had been about to turn back, when he suddenly glimpsed a far-off speck that looked like daylight. At that moment, he had dropped the string and groped towards the speck of light. Reaching it, he had pushed his head and shoulders through a small hole. And there was the broad Mississippi River below!

An Eager Audience Hears Tom's Story.

"Just think," Tom added, "if it had happened at night, I wouldn't have seen that speck of daylight, and I wouldn't have explored that passage any more. So, I went back to Becky and broke the good news to her, but she told me not to bother her with such stuff, for she was tired, and she knew she was going to die. I talked and talked until I finally convinced her that I'd found an opening. Then she almost died with joy when I led her to that blue speck of daylight.

"We climbed out and sat beside the cave, crying with happiness until some men came along. I hailed them and told them our story. At first, they didn't believe me. They said it was a wild tale, but they took us home, fed us, and let us sleep for a few hours before bringing us back home."

Three days of toil and hunger in the cave were not to be shaken off at once, as Tom and Becky soon discovered. They were bedridden

Leaving the Cave

all of Wednesday and Thursday and seemed to grow more and more tired and worn all the time. Tom moved about a little on Thursday, was downtown on Friday, and was nearly as good as new by Saturday. But Becky did not leave her room until Sunday, and then she looked as if she had passed through a wasting illness.

Tom learned that Huck, too, was ill and was staying with Mr. Welsh and his sons. He went to visit his friend and was warned to keep still, not to excite Huck, and not to mention the incident with the Widow Douglas. Tom had already been told of Huck's brave act and about the discovery of a body in the river—a body identified as Injun Joe's partner. The man had obviously been drowned while trying to escape from the Welshes.

About two weeks after Tom's rescue from the cave, he stopped off to see Becky. Mr. Thatcher and some friends asked Tom if he

Tom Visits Huck.

wouldn't mind returning to the cave some-time. Tom said he thought he wouldn't mind it. It was then that Mr. Thatcher explained to Tom, "To prevent anyone else getting lost in the cave, I had the place sealed up and triple locked two weeks ago."

Tom turned white as a sheet.

"What's the matter, boy?" cried Mr. Thatcher. "Run, somebody! Get a glass of water!"

The water was brought and thrown into Tom's face.

"What's the matter?" repeated Mr. Thatcher.

"Injun Joe's in the cave!" whispered Tom.

"What's the Matter, Boy?"

Finding Injun Joe's Body

CHAPTER 18
Buried Treasure

Within minutes, the news had spread around town, and dozens of men were on their way to the cave with Tom and Mr. Thatcher.

When the cave door was unlocked, a sorrowful sight presented itself in the dim twilight. Injun Joe lay stretched upon the ground, dead, his face close to the crack of the door. It seemed as if his last moments had been spent searching for light and cheer from the outside world.

Tom was touched, for he knew through his own experience how this man must have suffered. Tom felt pity, but even more, he felt an incredible sense of relief and security. Injun Joe was dead. No longer would Tom's dreams be haunted by thoughts of Injun Joe's revenge. No longer would he tiptoe around, wondering when the man would seek him out for having saved Muff Potter's life.

Injun Joe's bowie knife lay close by. Its blade was broken in two from Injun Joe's unsuccessful attempts at chipping and hacking at the door which blocked the cave exit.

Ordinarily, one could find dozens of bits of candles left by tourists in the crevices of this path. But now there were none. Injun Joe must have searched them out and eaten them. He had probably also caught a few bats and had eaten them too, leaving only their claws. The man had starved to death.

The men in the search party buried Injun Joe near the mouth of the cave. People flocked there in boats and wagons from the

A Broken Bowie Knife

towns, villages, and farms for miles around. They brought their children and all sorts of food, making it more of a picnic than a funeral.

The morning after the funeral, Tom and Huck went to their secret place on the hill to have an important talk. Huck had learned all about Tom's adventure from Mr. Welsh and the Widow Douglas, and now Huck wanted to explain to Tom all that had happened to him.

"I was standing watch outside the tavern, Tom, just like we agreed, and I followed Injun Joe and his partner when they left. I overheard their terrible plans for the Widow Douglas, so I ran to Mr. Welsh and begged him to save her."

"That was great, Huck!" said Tom. "But why didn't you want anyone to know how brave you were?"

"Because even though the Widow Douglas

People Come from Miles Around.

was saved, Injun Joe had escaped."

Tom nodded. He understood exactly how Huck had felt. But that was done, and Tom wanted to discuss the subject that had been on his mind for weeks—the treasure.

"Huck," he said, "that money was never in room number two at the tavern."

"What!" Huck searched his friend's face for some sort of clue. "Tom, have you got on the track of that money again?"

"Huck, it's in the cave!"

Huck's eyes blazed. "Say it again, Tom," he cried.

"The money's in the cave."

"Tom, are you serious? Do you promise you aren't kidding about this?"

"I'm serious, Huck. Will you go in the cave with me and help get it out?"

"You bet I will! . . . That is, I will, if we can do it without getting lost."

"Huck, we can do it without the least little

"The Money's in the Cave!"

bit of trouble. I promise you that. We'll need some bread and meat, a few strong bags, and three balls of kite string. Also, plenty of matches."

The boys gathered their supplies and, a little after noon, they got underway. When they were close to the opposite shore of the river, Tom pointed high up on the hillside and said, "Now you see this bluff? It looks like all the others, but there's a small white mark up there. See it, Huck? That's one of my marks. We'll get ashore now."

The boys pulled the raft on shore, and Tom showed Huck the tiny cave opening hidden behind a thick clump of bushes. Huck was impressed. The hole would have been impossible to find without Tom.

They climbed through the hole and entered the cave. Tom took the lead, and they made their way to the far end of the tunnel. As they passed the spring, Tom felt a shudder go

Going Ashore

through him. He showed Huck the fragment of candlewick perched on a lump of clay against the wall, and he described how he and Becky had sat there watching the flame struggle and die.

The boys continued on through another corridor, talking only in whispers, until they reached the ledge. Then Tom raised his candle high in the air and tugged at Huck's sleeve. "Now I'll show you something," said Tom. "Look as far around the corner as you can. Do you see that? There, on the big rock, written with ashes?"

"Tom, it's a cross!"

"Now, where's your number two? Under the cross, right?"

Huck stared at the cross a while, then said with a shaky voice, "Tom, let's get out of here!"

But Tom was the cool voice of reason. He slowly explained to Huck that there were no

"It's a Cross!"

ghosts in the cave. "Injun Joe is dead," he reminded Huck, "and we've both suffered enough looking for the treasure. Now that we're so close, it's silly to be afraid." Tom managed to convince Huck that the treasure was rightfully theirs.

At the base of a rock, they saw signs of activity—a blanket, some tools, and a piece of bacon rind—but no metal treasure chest.

"He said under the cross," whispered Huck. "Well, this comes nearest to being under the cross. It can't be under the rock itself, because that sets on solid clay ground."

They searched everywhere around the rock, then sat down discouraged. Huck had no ideas, but Tom was thinking and planning all the while he sat.

"Look there, Huck! There's footprints and some candle grease on the clay on one side of this rock, but not on the other sides. Now what's that for? I bet you the money *is* under

Footprints and Candle Grease

the rock. I'm going to dig in the clay."

They both began to scratch and dig, and after two hours they uncovered some boards. Once the boards were removed, they discovered a whole new corridor which led under the rock. They followed the path until it turned a curve.

Tom stopped suddenly and exclaimed, "Huck, I've found it! Here's the treasure."

It *was* the treasure box, sure enough. Tom lifted the lid, and Huck scooped up the tarnished coins with his clay-filled hands.

"We're rich, Tom! We really are!"

For a few moments, the boys just stood and looked at their treasure. Soon, they began putting the money into the bags and carrying it out of the cave.

When they emerged from the cave into the clump of bushes, they looked around to make sure all was clear. After a short rest for lunch, the boys loaded their raft and pushed out into

"We're Rich!"

the river. The sun was dipping toward the horizon as they left the shore, and by the time they landed, it was already dark.

"Now, Huck," said Tom, "we'll hide the money in the loft of the Widow's woodshed. I'll come up in the morning, and we'll count it and divide it. Then we'll hunt up a place out in the woods for it where it will be safe. But for now, just you lay quiet here and watch the stuff while I run and find a wagon. I'll only be gone a minute."

Tom disappeared, but soon returned with the wagon. They put the sacks of money into it and started off, dragging their treasure behind them.

As the boys passed Mr. Welsh's house, the old man stepped out and called, "Is that you, Huck . . . and you, Tom? Come along with me. Everyone is waiting."

Mr. Welsh helped them pull the wagon a short ways down the road, and they parked

Dragging the Treasure to a Safe Place

it outside the Widow Douglas' house. There was a party going on inside. The Thatchers, the Harpers, Aunt Polly, and just about everybody of importance was there. The Widow greeted the boys as heartily as anyone could greet two such ragged, dirty-looking young men who were covered with clay and candle grease from their latest adventure. Aunt Polly blushed and frowned, then shook her head at Tom. But before she had a chance to say a word, Mr. Welsh began explaining how he had stumbled on Tom and Huck right at his door. "So I just brought them along," he added.

"And you did right," said the Widow. "Come with me, boys." She took Tom and Huck to a bedroom and added, "Now wash and dress yourselves. Here are two new suits of clothes with shirts and socks and everything you'll need. We'll wait for you downstairs. Come down when you're ready."

The Widow Douglas Greets the Boys.

Hucks Wants to Get Away.

CHAPTER 19
A Home for Huck

Huck looked at the clothes, then at Tom, and said, "Tom, we can get out of here if we can find a rope. The window isn't too high up."

"What do you want to get away for?" asked Tom.

"Well, I'm not used to that kind of a crowd. I can't stand it. I'm not going down there, Tom."

"Oh, don't worry, Huck! It's nothing. I'll take care of you."

Then Sid entered the room and told Tom

and Huck that the party had been planned for a special reason—Mr. Welsh intended to tell everyone that it was Huck who had saved the Widow's life. And then the Widow was going to announce some secret.

"I don't know what the secret is," added Sid, "but I do know that Mr. Welsh wants Huck to be there to hear it."

Later, when the Widow's guests were at the supper table and a dozen children were propped up at little side tables, Mr. Welsh rose to make his speech. He thanked the Widow for the dinner she was giving in honor of his sons and himself. "But," he added, "there is another person whose modesty will not permit him to reveal his part in this brave rescue." Then, in his finest dramatic manner, Mr. Welsh told the secret about Huck's share in the adventure.

Widow Douglas heaped compliments and thanks on Huck. Everyone was looking at

Mr. Welsh Praises Huck.

him, but poor Huck was just sitting there, squirming in his new and very uncomfortable suit.

Then the Widow announced that she meant to give Huck a home under her roof and have him educated. She added that when she could spare the money, she would start him in business in a modest way.

Tom saw that his chance had come. "Huck doesn't need money," he announced. "Huck is rich."

Only respect for the Widow stopped everyone from laughing out loud at Tom's foolish words. Huck, *rich*?

"Huck's got money," continued Tom. "Maybe you don't believe it, but he's got lots of it. Oh, you needn't smile. I guess I'll have to show you. Just wait a minute."

Tom ran outside. The guests looked at each other with a confused interest. Huck sat frozen to his seat. He couldn't bring himself to

Tom Displays the Treasure.

utter a word.

Tom entered, struggling with the weight of the sacks. He poured the mass of yellow coins onto the table and cried, "There! What did I tell you? Half of it's Huck's and half of it's mine!"

The spectacle took everyone's breath away. But in moments, they were all demanding an explanation.

Tom told the long, but interesting story, while everyone listened in silence. When he was finished, the money was counted. The sum amounted to a little over *twelve thousand dollars*! It was more money than anyone present had ever seen before.

"Huck Is Rich."

Tom and Huck Are Stars.

CHAPTER 20
Respectable Huck Joins the Gang

Tom and Huck's windfall caused quite a stir in the little town. It was talked about, gloated over, and glorified until the real story was pale and uninteresting compared to the myth created by the constant gossip.

Whenever Tom and Huck appeared, they were stared at and admired. They were stars. Everywhere they went, they were followed. Everything they said was listened to with sharp interest and repeated.

Widow Douglas put Huck's money in the bank for him, and Aunt Polly did the same with Tom's share. Each boy had an income now. Although it was only a dollar a day, to Tom and Huck it was a fortune.

Huck Finn's wealth and the fact that he was now under the Widow Douglas' protection introduced him to a whole new world. But for Huck, it was a world he wished he had never known. The Widow's servants kept him clean and neat, combed and brushed. He had to eat with a knife and fork, and he had to use a napkin, cup, and plate. The Widow even forced him to go to church.

Huck bravely bore these miseries for three weeks, and then one day he ran away. For three days, everyone hunted for him.

Early on the fourth morning, Tom wisely went poking around the abandoned slaughterhouse—one of Huck's earlier favorite hiding places. Sure enough, Huck was there. He was wearing his old rags and looked unkempt and uncombed.

Tom Finds Huck's Hiding Place.

When Tom told him how worried everyone was over his disappearance, Huck said, "Don't talk about it, Tom. I've tried that life, and it doesn't work. It isn't for me. The Widow was good to me, but I can't live like she does. She makes me dress and wash and do everthing at a special time, and I'm just not used to living that way."

Tom tried to convince Huck that he would learn to like his new life, but it seemed hopeless. Then Tom thought of a plan to get Huck to stay with the Widow.

"Look here, Huck," he said. "We're going to form that gang we talked about back at the cave. But we can't let you join if you aren't respectable."

Huck was sad for a moment. "Can't you let me in, Tom?" he asked. "Didn't you let me play pirate?"

"Yes, but this is much more high-toned than a gang of pirates," said Tom.

Huck Refuses to Return to the Widow.

"Now, Tom, haven't we always been friends?" pleaded Huck. "You wouldn't leave me out, would you?"

"Huck, I wouldn't want to, and I *don't* want to, but what would people say? Why, they'd say, 'Mph! Tom Sawyer's gang! Pretty low characters in it,' and they'd mean *you*, Huck. You wouldn't like that, and neither would I."

Huck was silent for a long time. He had been used to living his own way for so many years, but now everything was different. Both the Widow and Tom wanted him to change. Maybe it wouldn't be so bad after all.

"Well, I'll go back to the Widow for a month and tackle it and see if I can stand it, but only if you let me belong to the gang, Tom."

So Tom and Huck walked arm and arm towards the Widow's big house on the hill. And as they walked, they planned all sorts of new adventures.

Planning New Adventures